I0537718

Xenotech
First Contact Day

A Story of the Galactic Free Trade Association

Adventures in the
Galactic Free Trade Association
universe continue in:

Xenotech Rising

Xenotech Queen's Gambit

and

Xenotech What Happens

soon to be followed by

Xenotech General Mayhem

coming in Q4 2016

Sign up for the Xenotech Support mailing list at
XenotechSupport.com to get advance notice
of new publications and receive a link to a
bonus short story.

Please visit

www.XenotechSupport.com

for more details about
the universe of Xenotech Support
and the Galactic Free Trade Association

To my wife, Amy Guildroy,
for her help with the ending.

With appreciation for Michelle Hartz,
who suggested the original title,
and Robert A. Heinlein
who inspired us all.

Previously released in Kindle format as:
The Man Who Sold the Earth

Copyright © 2015 by Paul David Schroeder

Cover design by Dan Paulson

ISBN: 978-0-9978319-0-0

Spiral Arm Press
1725 Carlington Court
Grayson, GA 30017
www.spiralarmpress.com

First Contact Day

"The fault, dear Brutus, is not in our stars,
but in ourselves."
– William Shakespeare, *Julius Caesar*

First contact was not made when a spaceship landed on the White House lawn, but when a three-alien delegation teleported into the office of the most powerful man in the world. The visitors had timed it well, arriving at the beginning of a half-hour block the great man had reserved for a restorative mid-day power nap.

"What can JPMorgan Chase do to help you gentlebeings?" said the chairman.

"We come in peace," said the tallest of the visitors, a lean, tiger-striped seven foot humanoid.

"Live long and prosper," said the shortest alien, a three-foot pyramid with an eye at the apex of each side.

"Klaatu barada…" began the third alien, a round, red-skinned being with a beard made of long, white, manipulative tentacles who looked like a caricature of Santa Claus.

"Cut the crap," said the chairman.

"Right," said the tallest alien. "We're from the Galactic Free Trade Association and we want to cut you in."

"I see," said the chairman. "What's in it for me?"

"Unlimited, practically free energy," said the pyramid alien.

So much for ExxonMobil, thought the chairman.

"The cure for cancer," said the Santa Claus alien.

Ditto for Pfizer and Hospital Corporation of America.

The tall alien spoke. "Warp drives and…" —the alien moved its hands from its head to its knees to indicate Star Trek's transporter special effect—"teleportation."

I

Sell transportation stocks short.

"And what could *you* possibly want from *us*?"

The three aliens looked at each other and by unspoken consensus the pyramid took the lead in answering.

"We're never exactly sure what will prove popular in Galactic markets," it said, "but we know that free trade is always beneficial to all participants."

"Tell it to the Native Americans," said the chairman. "You know about them?"

"Yes," said the Santa. "We've been studying Earth for a long time."

"So you want to come to our planet and buy our valuables for twenty-four dollars in beads and trinkets?"

"The cure for cancer is hardly wampum," said the pyramid.

"And you'd get access to our Galactic stock market databases so you could see the value of your trade goods and could bargain with us as an equal," said the tall alien.

"It wouldn't be fair, otherwise," said the pyramid.

Fair. The chairman gave a mental snort. *This is business.*

"Don't treat me like a child," said the chairman.

The tall, furred, tiger-striped alien glanced at the ceiling for a moment as if to say, "That's *not* what we we're doing," then looked directly at the chairman and gave a wry smile. It was exactly what they were doing.

"What commodities are you looking for?" said the chairman. "If you tell me, I'll help you get them—at a good price."

"We're rather fond of chocolate," said the red-skinned, white tentacle-bearded alien.

"And maple syrup," said the pyramid.

"And Jelly Belly candies," said the tall alien. "Yum." The look on the alien's face made it clear it had already sampled the flavorful confections.

The chairman made mental notes. *Buy Hershey and Nestle shares. Get options on sugar maple stands in Vermont, Quebec and Ontario. Acquire the Jelly Belly Candy Company.*

"Got it," said the chairman. "You like sweets. What else?"

"We're also rather fond of Gilbert & Sullivan," said the Santa. It started singing. *"I am the captain of the Pin-a-fore..."*

The other two aliens joined in. *"And a right good captain too!"*

"GaFTA member species *love* Gilbert & Sullivan," said the tall alien. "Almost as much as broadcasts of legisla..."

"Shush," said the pyramid.

"What's GaFTA?" said the chairman.

"It's a shortened way of referring to the Galactic Free Trade Association," the pyramid replied.

"Oh, right. We do that, too. It helps sell the politicians—like NAFTA. If we had a good acronym like that we'd have an easier time selling Congress on the Trans-Pacific Partnership Agreement."

"Speaking of Congress," said the tall alien.

"Don't worry about them," said the chairman. "They won't be a problem. I'll take care of it. They owe me."

"That's not what I meant," answered the tall alien. "GaFTA member species are interested in following the deliberations of Earth's legislative bodies to become better informed citizens and fully acquaint themselves with the issues important to our newest member planet."

"That's a pile of horse puckey, bucko," said the chairman. "You can't even *say* it with a straight face."

Somehow, the tall alien resembling a bipedal tiger managed to look sheepish.

"I thought so," said the chairman, who seemed to pause and restart. "But I'm being a poor host. Would any of you gentlebeings like some sort of refreshment? Coffee? Tea? Water? I don't know what works with your biochemistry."

"Hot chocolate for me," said the pyramid.

"And for me," said the Santa.

"I'll take the cream you would have put in my coffee," said the tall alien.

The chairman took note that its preference, along with its appearance, was feline. He pushed a button on his ornate gold speaker phone.

"George, could you bring a couple of hot chocolates and a large cup of cream to my office for my guests, please? And an espresso for me—it's going to be a long day."

A medium tenor voice answered.

"Your guests, sir? I thought you were 'researching the markets.'"

His personal secretary was using their code for "restorative midday power nap."

"They must have come in while you were away from your desk," said the chairman.

"But I never left my…"

"Just bring the drinks, George."

"Yes, sir."

"And keep a firm hold on the tray..."

"Whatever you say, sir. It won't be a moment."

The chairman pressed the button again to turn off the speaker function and focused on his guests.

"I'd appreciate a few days to keep the knowledge of your arrival and invitation to myself," he said. "That way I can work behind the scenes to reduce potential problems for the global economy."

"You mean you want time to conduct some discreet insider trading," said the tall alien, looking pleased about scoring points back on the chairman.

"No, no," said the pyramid. "That simply won't do. It wouldn't be *fair* to give you too much of a head start. The press conference needs to be held this afternoon."

"This afternoon!" said the chairman. His expression resembled the one he'd had when an employee in the U.K. nicknamed "The Orca" had lost more than six billion dollars in unauthorized derivatives trading. "At least tell me we can wait until after the market closes."

"Of course," said the Santa. "But that only gives you a couple of hours to set things up."

"I guess we could hold it in the lobby," said the chairman. *Oh crap,* he thought. *Today would have to be April first.*

"We were thinking Times Square," said the pyramid.

"The stage is still up from the America's Got Talent special last night," said the Santa. "I really liked the talking dog."

A knock on the chairman's oak-paneled door saved him from having to respond to the Santa alien's comment.

"Come in."

George entered, carrying a silver tray with three large bank logo mugs and a small porcelain cup. Guests didn't get the Limoges china cups unless their net worth was known and north of five hundred million. A serving spoon and a glass bowl filled with whipped cream resting in a larger silver bowl filled with ice were next to the mugs. George gripped the tray tightly and didn't look at his boss or his guests until he'd put the tray down on a convenient marble-topped table.

"Would you like me to serve, sir?" said George, who was a very well trained and well paid personal secretary.

Then he noticed the visitors, and bowed, thinking he'd really blown it by not using the good china.

"I didn't know if you'd like whipped cream with your hot chocolate," he said, "so I brought some along just in case."

"I like mini-marshmallows," said the Santa, *sotto voce.*

"Shush," said the pyramid. "Whipped cream for both of us, thank you."

George handed the tall alien its mug and added generous dollops of whipped cream to the other mugs before serving them.

He managed to keep it together when the pyramid used a tentacle extruded from below one of its three mouths to grasp its mug. The Santa alien wasn't so bad, except when its beard tentacles writhed, which they did when inhaling the rich, sweet, complex smell of the imported Harrod's hot chocolate and the freshly-made whipped cream.

"Ahhhh," said the Santa, inclining its head toward George. "I'm sure this will taste as good as it smells."

The pyramid sipped its hot chocolate.

"It's delicious. Thank you," it said.

"It would be even better with mini-marshmallows," said the Santa.

"Shush," said the pyramid, a bit more insistently.

The tall alien just smiled, showing canines that looked less threatening with a cream mustache.

"I'm glad you like your drinks, good gentles," said George. He noted that the chairman had grabbed his cup of espresso while he was working on the whipped cream.

"I'll leave you to your discussions. Let me know if you need anything."

George headed for the door.

"Just a moment," said the chairman. "Stay right here. I need your help."

George cleared his throat and looked at the chairman expectantly. He cleared his throat again.

"Are you coming down with something, George?" said the chairman.

"No," said the pyramid. "He's waiting to be introduced."

"Come to think of it, so am I," said the chairman. "I expect you know who I am."

"Your reputation precedes you," said the pyramid. "I am Charles Maurice de Talleyrand-Périgord, envoy extraordinary and minister plenipotentiary to Earth from the Galactic Free Trade Association."

The chairman looked thoughtful. *Wasn't Talleyrand Napoleon's chief diplomat? Is the pyramid pulling my leg?*

"Very pleased to meet you," said the chairman, extending his hand. The end of another one of the pyramid's tentacles flattened out and gave him five, or what might, in other circumstances, have been five, since the pyramid didn't have fingers.

George shook hands as well.

"Very pleased to meet you, too," he said.

"I'm a Pyr," said the pyramid.

"A Purr?" said George. "Like a cat?"

"No, like the ancient pointy things near Cairo. But it sounds like a long wooden structure extending into the ocean that you fish from—or a member of the British House of Lords."

"Oh. A *Pyr*," said George. "Got it."

"I know my full name is a mouthful," said the Pyr. "The custom for my species is to name themselves after beings they admire that fit with their roles and responsibilities. I understand that Talleyrand was a good diplomat, so I named myself for him."

"Okay," said George, who got it, but still didn't quite *get* it.

"For formal occasions my full name is recommended," said the Pyr, "but for everyday conversations, you can call me Chuck. I'm male, by the way, that's why I chose a man's name. Gender seems to matter a lot on Earth. Our females have four sides, not three."

The chairman nodded and smiled on automatic pilot.

"Thanks, Chuck. Good to know," he said. "And who are the other members of your delegation?"

"They can introduce themselves."

The Santa alien stepped forward.

"My people are known as Nicósns, from the planet Nicós. I am also male and my name is Jannosh. Our species uses numeric identifiers rather than last names, sort of like personal IP addresses, so I'll spare you my sixty-four character designation."

"Pleased to meet you, Jannosh," said the chairman and George in turn, glad that the Nicósn, at least, had human-like hands.

Now it was the tall alien's turn. The humans watched as a long tongue circled and wiped the excess cream from around the being's tooth-filled mouth.

"My name is Murriym, and I'm a female from the planet Tigram." Her voice had the not unpleasant buzz of a big cat's growl.

"So you're Tigrams?" asked George.

"We couldn't make it that easy," said Murriym. "The demonym for my people is Tigrammath. That's also the word for our language."

"Tigram*math*," said George. "I *like* math."

"I expect our two species will get along just fine," said Murriym. "It's the Pyrs who are the true mathematical geniuses, though."

"You can always count on them," said Jannosh. Chuck snapped the Nicósn's knee with a chastising tentacle.

"Sorry," said Jannosh.

"Settle down," said the chairman. "We've got a lot of work to do. George, not a word about this to anyone else until the press conference. Call the mayor's office and get that stage reserved for four o'clock. If there's any problem, tell him he'll never forgive himself if he doesn't make this happen. We'll need major police presence as well. Tell him it will be like New Year's Eve. If you get push back, mention the word *Rosebud* and that should clear any obstacles. Notify the networks and ensure there's plenty of coverage. But *no* details."

"Yes, sir," said George, heading for his desk outside.

"Stop," said the chairman. "Nobody enters or leaves this room until we head out for the press conference. Make all your arrangements from here. If this leaks there will hell to pay."

"Right," said George, locking the CEO's office door from the inside and moving to his auxiliary workstation to the left of his boss's desk. He put on a headset and started making calls.

"And George," said the chairman, loud enough to be heard through the headphones. "Get me the president."

"The White House?"

"Good God, no," said the chairman. "The president of the Federal Reserve. She'd kill me if I didn't at least give her *some* warning about what's in store for the economy."

While George and the chairman were busy with logistical details for the press conference, the three aliens came together and spoke quietly.

"I *told* you we picked the best person for first contact," said the Pyr.

"You were right and I was wrong," said Jannosh the Nicósn. "I wanted to tell the President."

"But he would have had to tell the opposition and then imagine what sort of circus this would turn into," said the Pyr. "Can you imagine the impact we'll have on their immigration policy?"

"No politicians. That's the rule," said Murriym the Tigrammath.

"Right," said Chuck. "And one that's served us well."

"Isn't the head of the Federal Reserve a politician?" asked Jannosh.

"Only indirectly and not by training," said Murriym. "She's sort of halfway between a politician and a business person."

"And that makes it okay?" said Jannosh.

"Quiet," said the Pyr. "The chairman's making a video call."

George had gotten through two gatekeepers at the Fed with his usual efficiency and was ready to connect his boss with the Chairman of the Federal Reserve. He'd been told to make it a video call so that the head of the Fed could see his boss's body language.

"You're live, sir," said George.

The three aliens circled around behind the JPMorgan Chase chairman so they could follow the conversation but still remain off camera. A short-haired woman's face appeared on the screen.

"Are you sitting down?" said the bank chairman.

"Nice to see you, too," said the Fed chairman. "Of course I'm sitting down. I have to sit down for the camera to see me, according to my IT people. To what do I owe the honor of this unscheduled conversation?"

The two leaders were old friends, but they were also busy people whose schedules were managed with the precision of lawyers allocating billable hours.

"You need to have all the exchanges in the country suspend trading after four o'clock today," he said, "and have your counterparts do the same around the world."

The Fed chairman saw the look on his face and didn't say what she wanted to say—something on the order of *Have you gone mad?*"

"What do you know?"

"It's big. Second Coming big."

"I never took you for a religious man," she said.

"I'm not. It's not Jesus, but it's every bit as Earth-shattering. World markets and financial systems will go crazy after my press conference in Times Square at four o'clock."

"Thanks for the warning, I think," said the Fed chair. She tried to read his face on her monitor. "Can you give me a hint?"

"I'm not supposed to say anything to anybody before the announcement."

Chuck moved in front of the bank chairman and waved a tentacle at the camera.

"It's going to be big news," said the Pyr, waving two tentacles for emphasis. "I'd make the calls to suspend trading now." Then he glided back out of camera range.

The Fed chairman's eyes were wide and her mouth was open. Then she pulled herself together.

"If you're pulling a practical joke on April Fool's Day…"

"I'd never joke about something like this."

"What, never?" said Jannosh, popping his white beard-tentacled face in front of the camera for a moment.

"Well, hardly ever," said Murriym, doing the same from the other side with droll Tigrammath humor.

The Fed chairman's look of shock returned, doubled and redoubled. Then she spoke.

"I'll make the calls."

"Thank you," said the bank chairman. "April 1, 2015 will join July 20, 1969 as a date that changed the planet forever."

"What happened on July 20, 1969?"

"The moon landing."

"Oh, yeah, right."

"You'll make the calls?"

"As soon as I hang up."

"Thanks. Not a word about *why*—just make it happen."

"Understood. Uhura out." She cut the connection.

"Everyone's a comedian," said the bank chairman. He nodded at the alien trio. "The persuasive assist was appreciated."

"No problem," said the Pyr. "By the way, how do you plan to get us to the stage at Times Square without us being seen?"

"There's a private elevator from my office to the parking garage. We can restrict access to the level where my limo is parked and take you down that way."

"But how do we get from your limo to the stage?" said Murriym.

"George, send some interns down to that Islamic clothing store in Tribeca with a company credit card. Tell them to buy three chadors with head scarves and veils. One extra tall, one short and one medium. And have them pick up a long, plain black skirt, too."

The chairman looked at Murriym.

"Size eight," said the Tigrammath.

"Got that?"

"Got it," said George. "I'm also arranging a police escort so they'll be back in time."

"Smart," said the chairman. "What's the word from the networks?"

"All the majors will be there," said George, "and lots of little fish, too. Once they heard that something big was coming down, they all decided to send crews."

"Excellent," said his boss. "You want maximum exposure, right?"

"Yes," said Chuck. "'Damn the torpedoes, full speed ahead,' as a famous Terran named Perry said during an earlier example of first contact between civilizations."

"That was Admiral David Farragut, not Commodore Matthew Perry," said the chairman, who was something of a history buff. "If you're referring to opening Japan to trade with West, Perry said something more along the lines of 'open your borders to our trade or our battleships will pound the hell out of your capital.'"

"My apologies," said Chuck, "though in practice the sentiments are equivalent. Free trade is unstoppable."

"Does that mean you have space battleships hidden in orbit?"

"They don't need to be in orbit," said the little Pyr. "With congruent-tech wormhole drives they can be here in hours from the closer GaFTA planets. But we don't have battleships, just armed merchant vessels for protection from pirates. With unlimited free trade, we've evolved beyond warfare."

Yes, and there's a bridge to Brooklyn not far from here I'd like to sell you, thought the chairman.

"Fascinating. That does get us down to the particulars, though."

"What do you mean?"

"I'm holding a press conference in an hour and a half to announce first contact with not one, but three alien species who come bearing gifts, but I don't have any details about what you're putting on the table."

"You're connecting with far more than three alien species," said

Murriym. She was literally looking down at him. "There are 967 species in the Galactic Free Trade Association to date, and it's only Wednesday."

"You're not helping," said the chairman. "I've got to put together a press release and a speech for the news conference that will reassure the planet that this is just another business relationship for the companies of Earth—not the biggest thing to happen since the invention of fire. And I've got to figure out a perfect statement for the three of you."

"Don't worry," said Chuck. "We've done this before. I've got a script that's never failed."

"Let me see it," said the chairman.

"I sent it to your printer."

George was still on the phone arranging logistical details, so the chairman removed the warm sheets from the output tray himself.

"Hmmmm," he said, squinting slightly at the small print. "'We're from the Galactic Free Trade Association and we're here to help you.' Oh dear God."

"What?" said Chuck.

"If I let you say that, you'll be lucky to make it off the stage alive."

"I told you we should have had a Pâkk in the delegation for self-defense," Murriym whispered to Jannosh.

"I thought that's why *you* were here," Jannosh replied.

"In some parts of the United States the phrase 'We're from the government and we're here to help you' is considered highly offensive. In the rest of the country it's just considered funny. If you say it, you'll be crucified."

"Literally?" asked the Pyr. "Given my species' anatomy, that might be hard to do."

"Okay, be that way," said the chairman. "Do you have an orifice where waste leaves your body?"

"Yes, in the center of my base. It's surrounded by my mobility cilia."

"Good. Then I'll rephrase my statement. If I let you say that, you'll be impaled. Do you understand *impaled?*"

"Let me look it up."

The Pyr consulted a donut-shaped device he pulled from somewhere on his person. Lights flashed and symbols appeared on the unit's edge.

"Oh dear Euclid! We won't use that phrase at the press conference. We won't. We won't."

"Good, though we may release it afterward to defuse tension about your arrival," said the chairman. "Maybe I can get Think-Geek to make t-shirts."

The chairman watched the Pyr calm himself—at least that was how he translated the alien's reduced rate of trembling.

"What do you suggest we say?" said the little pyramid.

"First, tell me the full terms of the deal," said the chairman. "Once I understand, I can figure out how to share it with the public."

Air slowly whistled out of the Pyr somewhere—*spiracles?*—as if he was sighing.

"It's simple, really," Chuck said. "Like hundreds of other species, Terrans are now eligible for membership in the Galactic Free Trade Association."

"Why now?" asked the chairman.

"Because you've independently developed congruent technology."

"What?"

"Wormholes. Ways of connecting two separate points in space as if there was no intervening distance," said the Pyr. "It's how we get unlimited energy, raw materials, and faster than light travel."

"And teleportation," said Jannosh.

"Though that's mostly used for cargo," said Murriym. "There are still risks and unfortunate side effects related to teleporting complex matrices like sentient minds."

"Side effects?" said the chairman.

"A one in ten thousand chance of brain damage," said Chuck.

That explains a lot, thought the chairman.

"I haven't heard anything about our scientists creating wormholes," he said. "Something like that should be front page news."

Murriym stopped licking the fur on the back of her left hand and replied.

"Last Friday at 3:37 p.m. in Pittsburgh, Pennsylvania, Dr. Janet Yu and her team of researchers, academics from Carnegie Mellon working on a DARPA funded project with IBM, successfully used microchip technology to create the space time topological stresses needed to generate a wormhole."

"Last Friday?" said the chairman. "It's Wednesday. Why isn't it all over the Internet?"

"Due to Congressional budget cuts, the project was shut down at 5:00 p.m. Friday afternoon," said Jannosh. "They never had a chance to verify their results."

"How did *you* find out about it?" asked the chairman.

"Congruency detectors," said Chuck. "We've been monitoring Earth for some time."

"They're expensive, but worth it," said Jannosh.

"Wormholes," said the chairman. "I'd always thought it would be developing a warp drive."

"One gets you the other," said Murriym, licking the fur of her other hand.

Was that a nervous gesture? thought the chairman.

"George, find Dr. Janet Yu at Carnegie Mellon—PhD, not medical doctor—and get her on the phone right away. I need a human hero for this press conference and she's it."

"Yes, sir," said George, who was on the phone with the chief of the NYPD arranging crowd control. He expertly used his silent keyboard and an expensive executive support search app to find Janet Yu's personal cell phone number and call it.

"Doctor Yu?" said George, taking advantage of a lull in the conversation with the police chief, "This is the executive secretary for the chairman of JPMorgan Chase. Do you have a few minutes to speak with him?"

George could hear crowd sounds and children's voices in the background.

"I guess so," said a puzzled contralto from the other end of the line.

"I'll connect you now," said George. He waved to get the chairman's attention. "Line two."

The chairman picked up his handset.

"Dr. Yu, this is the chairman of JPMorgan Chase. Are you sitting down?"

"No, I'm standing in the Hershey's Chocolate World store in Times Square trying to ride herd on my children. Put that down!"

"What?" said the chairman.

"Not you," said Dr. Yu, "my son. He's about to pull over a Reese's Pieces display. I'll be right back."

The chairman could hear dozens of cross-garbled conversations. Then he heard a crash and a sound like ten thousand poker chips being dumped on the floor.

"Sorry about that. I'll pay for it," the chairman heard Dr. Yu say. Then she was back on the line. "I was too late," she said.

"Are you the Dr. Janet Yu who is doing DARPA research with Carnegie Mellon and IBM?"

"I was until five o'clock on Friday. Now I'm just a tourist."

"Great. I'm glad to hear you're in New York. You're about to become world famous."

The chairman heard her talking, but not to him.

"How much? Three hundred dollars? You're kidding me."

Then she came back.

"Mister, I don't know if you are who you *say* you are, but you just cost me three hundred dollars I really didn't want to spend. Anthony, stop eating those off the floor! Jeanette, grab your brother."

"How would you like three hundred *thousand* dollars deposited in your bank account in the next five minutes?" said the chairman.

"Say what? Is this a phishing attempt? I'm not giving you my bank account number no matter *who* you say you are."

"George," said the chairman.

George was already typing.

"As if I needed you to tell me," said the chairman to himself.

"There you are, Tony! Where were you?" said Dr. Yu. "Pick up *your* son. Elizabeth, Jeanette, stand next to your father and be good. Don't step on the candy! I'll be with you as soon as I get off the phone."

The chairman heard subdued crunching sounds under the general hubbub of Hershey's Chocolate World.

"What do you want?"

"I want to talk to you—privately—about the implications of your research. If you and your family would walk a block south on Broadway and go to the lobby of the New York Marriott Marquis at 47th Street, you'll find I've reserved a suite in your name. I'll meet you there with some friends of mine in less than an hour. Have a nice snack from room service on me."

"I'm not doing *anything* just because somebody claiming to be a corporate big shot says so."

"Check your bank balance."

George was already making arrangements at the hotel.

"Holy sh…" Then Dr. Yu remembered her children were in earshot. "Wow. Okay then."

"And there's plenty more where that came from to help fund you."

"The Marriott Marquis. Broadway and 47th. Room service. Got it."

"Thank you, Dr. Yu," said the chairman. "I knew you were quick on the uptake. I'll make arrangements to have your luggage moved from your current hotel to the Marquis."

"Thank you. We're staying at the…"

"I know where you're staying," said the chairman, nodding at George, who nodded back. "And we'll make arrangements for 24/7 security for you as well. Don't be alarmed if there are guards outside your suite."

"It's big, then?" said Janet.

"You have no idea," said the chairman. "But you will. Soon."

He hung up.

"Did you get all that, George?"

"Got it, boss. If you want to talk to Dr. Yu first, we're going to have to leave now."

"But when am I going to have a chance to write the press release and prepare my speech?"

"I'll take care of it," said George. "My assistant says the interns just dropped off the disguises."

"Excellent," said the chairman. "Let's grab them, get our guests properly dressed, and head for Times Square."

George returned with four large shopping bags. With the chairman's help, he got all three of the alien diplomats dressed from head to toe, or apex to mobility cilia in the Pyr's case. George had wisely instructed the interns to pick up a Styrofoam wig display head and Chuck used one of his tentacles to hold the head above the top of his body so that he looked more like a portly Saudi princess than a dumpy Dalek. Two other tentacles served as shoulders and gave the robes something to hang on. George offered to cut eye holes so the Pyr could see, but Chuck said he'd just extend an eye stalk so he could look through his veil. Murriym the Tigrammath needed the long, black skirt for full coverage—the chador alone only came down to her knees. The chairman's mind wandered and he wondered if Tigrammaths played basketball. George switched from his desktop to a more portable tablet computer so he could continue working his magic, then the five of them took the chairman's private elevator to the parking garage.

"I've cleared the level where the limousine is waiting," said George. "We'll pick up our police escort at the top of the ramp."

It was hard to tell through all the fabric, but the chairman got the distinct idea that the aliens were enjoying their adventure. He was concerned about how Chuck was going to get into the limo, but the little Pyr leaned back, shuffled forward on his rear cilia, and dropped his front inside the vehicle. The rest of him followed easily. Jannosh had no problem climbing in, but getting Murriym inside was more of a production. The chairman knew NBA players and they preferred limos based on SUVs, not stretch Lincolns, because they were higher off the ground and had more head room. The Tigrammath bent down and crawled into the limo, then sprawled at the far end of the passenger compartment, taking up four seats. The chairman entered, followed by George, who used the intercom to tell the driver they were all aboard.

The limo navigated the turns inside the parking garage smoothly then emerged into the spring sunshine to meet its escort, two marked NYPD patrol cars and a pair of motorcycle officers. The engines on the mounted officers' big Harley-Davidsons growled and blue lights on poles behind them began to rotate. They were joined by the light bars on the squad cars, but they didn't turn on their sirens. The mayor was adamant about keeping noise pollution to a minimum. They went half a block south on Park Avenue then turned right on 47th Street. At mid-afternoon on a Wednesday, traffic was bad—and all the television crews heading for or setting up at Times Square made it even worse. The police escort helped, but with the streets nearly gridlocked, there was nowhere for vehicles to move out of the way.

The aliens were staring out the windows. The chairman knew they'd been observing Earth for many years, but he sensed that this was the first time any of them had ever seen Manhattan from street level.

"After the press conference, could we see *The Lion King?*" asked Murriym.

"I want to see *Wicked,*" said Jannosh.

"And I want to see *Les Mis,*" said Chuck. *"Do you hear the people sing,"* he began in a strong tenor voice.

"I could probably buy out the theater for a private showing of *Mamma Mia,*" said George, quickly.

"Yeah," said all three aliens in unison. "That would be great."

"I think we need to wait and see how the world reacts to the announcement," said the chairman.

"True," said the Pyr. All three aliens looked subdued.

Have any of them ever done this before? thought the chairman.

After fifteen minutes they'd only traveled two long blocks from Park to Sixth Avenue. Then they sat. The intersection was blocked by a truck from Weasel News that insisted it had the right of way to turn south on Sixth when everyone in greater New York knew that avenue was one way north.

"George?" said the chairman, looking pointedly at his ninety-five thousand dollar Patek Philippe watch.

"The grid is well and truly locked," said George. "We're going to have to walk the last block and a half."

"You're kidding," said his boss. "We can't let our guests be seen in public before the press conference."

"This is New York," said George. "No one will give them a second look."

The chairman stroked his chin.

"You're probably right," he said. "Would any of you have any problems walking less than a quarter of a mile from here to the hotel?"

"How far is that in galmets?" asked Jannosh.

"Seven and a half," said Murriym.

"That shouldn't be a problem for any of us," said Chuck. "We're young and healthy members of our respective species."

"Everybody out of the car," said the chairman.

George went first and helped escort Chuck, Jannosh and Murriym to the sidewalk on the south side of 47th. He took the rear while the chairman led them through the intersection of Sixth and 47th and headed toward Times Square. Every now and then he had to tug on the robes of one of the aliens when they stopped to rubberneck and play the ultimate visitors from out of town. The chairman figured that two men in business suits with three women in traditional Islamic dress might be considered just a couple of brothers from Qatar seeing the Big Apple with their wives. A small, yappy dog tugged an older woman in a stylish pantsuit toward Murriym as it tried to tell the Tigrammath who was in charge on this planet, but a low growl from the seven-foot alien made the dominance hierarchy explicit. George tried to dissuade Chuck from buying a bag of roasted nuts from a street vendor at the corner of 47th and Seventh, then gave in and bought him a bag of candy-coated almonds to take along to the hotel.

"How many tentacles do you *have*?" George asked Chuck after the little alien grabbed the bag of almonds and hid it under his robes.

"As many as I need," said Chuck.

"Right," said George.

Jannosh didn't get into any trouble, but he kept stopping to take in all the smells of Times Square with his beard tentacles. Finally they crossed Broadway and reached the hotel. After overcoming the challenge of the aliens learning how to operate a revolving door, they were met by a pair of armed guards who escorted them to the elevators and followed them up to the suite George had booked for Dr. Yu and her family. Two other guards were on duty waiting for them. Before they could enter, a messenger came running down the hallway carrying a large, bulging FedEx Office bag with a folding closure. The guards reached for their weapons but George stopped them before they could draw.

"This is for me," George said, taking the bag and handing the messenger a twenty.

The chairman saw the look on his secretary's face and smiled. That look meant a pleasant surprise was in store. He knocked on the door.

"Dr. Yu?"

"Call me Janet," she said, opening the door wide. "Come in and meet my family."

"Excellent," said the chairman. All five of them trooped into the roomy luxury suite. The guards maintained their positions outside. George and the chairman introduced themselves and Janet presented her husband, Dr. Anthony Obi, and their three children, Jeanette, Elizabeth and Anthony, Jr., ages 10, 8 and 6. The chairman shook hands with everyone, including the children. Anthony, Jr. shook with a serious look on his face, but stared at the robed aliens as if he could see right through their chadors.

Dr. Yu was a slim, somewhat worn down Asian woman in her late thirties. She was about five foot seven with short, straight black hair and dark eyes that suggested hidden depths. Her husband was about the same age and three inches taller with short, curly black hair. His dark eyes seemed full of hidden amusement. From his last name and skin color, the chairman guessed he was first or second generation Nigerian. He'd hired a lot of Nigerians with doctorates in math when he was running the bank's analytics division and recognized his Igbo last name.

"How did the two of you meet?" he asked.

"In grad school at Stanford," said Janet.

Anthony, Jr. couldn't stay silent. The three robed figures had pointedly *not* been introduced and he needed to know who they were right *now.*

"Who are *they?*" he said.

"Shush," said his mother and Chuck simultaneously.

The not-quite-human voice from under the Pyr's robes did what his mother's instruction could not. Anthony, Jr. stepped back and hid behind his sisters. He didn't seem frightened, just confused.

"Please take off your robes," said the chairman.

The alien trio complied. Dr. Yu's family just stood there, eyes wide, but the first person on Earth to create a congruency didn't hesitate.

"Hi! I'm Janet. Pleased to meet you," she said to the smallest alien.

"Chuck," said the little Pyr, extending a flattened tentacle. "I'm honored to meet such a distinguished Terran scientist."

"Please tell that to my tenure committee," said Janet.

"You're the reason they're here, Dr. Yu," said the chairman. "They say that your wormhole discovery is what made Earth eligible for membership in the Galactic Free Trade Association."

"Now I'm the one who's honored," said Janet. She looked shaken. "That's why you've hired the armed guards?"

"You're going to be a very important person," said the chairman. "You and your family need to be protected. There are a lot of nuts out there."

"Thank you," said Janet.

"Excuse me," said a small voice.

Anthony, Jr. had found his courage and stepped around his sisters.

"I'm Anthony," he said. "It's nice to meet you, Mr. Chuck."

"Nice to meet you too," said the Pyr, who wasn't that much taller than the six year old.

"Are you an E.T.?" asked the boy.

"An extraterrestrial," prompted George.

"I guess I am," said Chuck. "I'm from a planet a long way from Earth."

"Then you should have these," said Anthony, pulling a handful of Reese's Pieces of dubious provenance from the pocket of his jeans. "E.T.s like them."

"I will treasure them always as a gift between our two species," said the Pyr, trying out his best flowery diplomatic language.

"You're supposed to eat them," said the boy.

"I wouldn't if I were you," said his older sister Jeanette.

"He got them off the floor," said his other sister Elizabeth.

"It's the thought that counts," said Dr. Obi, finding his voice and his manners. "You can keep those as an intercultural exchange artifact, but if you're going to eat any of them, I'd go with these." He handed Chuck a small unopened orange bag of the candies that he'd found in a pocket of his jacket. They were his son's favorite.

"Thanks," said Chuck, stowing the loose pieces somewhere on his person. He opened the package and passed out a few of the more sanitary candies to his compatriots.

"They're good," said Murriym.

"Not as good as chocolate," said Jannosh.

"*Your* gift is also appreciated, Dr. Obi," cut in Chuck. "Let me introduce my companions."

Introductions and species designations were made all around. Elizabeth wanted to touch Jannosh's beard tentacles and marveled at his bright red skin. Eight was a good age to be fascinated by an alien who looked like Santa Claus, even in April. Jeanette gravitated to Murriym and asked permission to pet the Tigrammath's fur.

"Oooo, it's soft, like a kitten's," she said.

"I use a full body cream rinse every day," said Murriym.

Anthony, Jr., pleased to have someone closer to his size to talk to, told Chuck a joke.

"Why is six afraid of seven?" he said.

"I have no idea," said the Pyr, who had the outstanding mathematical talent common to all members of his species. "Is *afraid* some new algebraic operator?"

"You're supposed to say, 'I don't know. Why?'" said the boy.

Chuck played along.

"I don't know. Why?"

"Because seven ate nine."

The Pyr started to shake and emit high-pitched *meeps* that frightened the boy at first until he realized the alien was laughing. In fact, Chuck was laughing so hard that moisture began to leak from all three of his eyes and he needed to wipe drool from his mouths with his tentacles.

"What's the big deal?" asked the chairman.

"It's a numeric pun," said the Pyr. "Unique in my experience. Number sense is innate to Pyrs, so we just don't think that way. But once I heard it I thought it was hilarious."

"If you say so," said the chairman.

"Anthony," said the Pyr, "if you give me permission to turn the video transcript of your joke into something to sell, I promise that it will go viral on my home world and you will be a very rich little boy."

Anthony, Sr. and Janet looked at Chuck.

"If your parents approve, of course," said the Pyr, contritely.

"College fund?" said Dr. Obi to his wife.

"Works for me," she said. "But I'll want to review the contract."

"I'll see to it," said Chuck.

"Video transcript?" said George.

"Have a candy-coated almond," said Chuck to Anthony, Jr.

"Can we get down to business," said the chairman. "We're running out of time."

There was a chorus of assents from the humans and noises that could be interpreted as such from the aliens. Everyone sat down on chairs arranged in a semicircle around the suite's functional, but not currently functioning fire place, except for the chairman, who stood, and Chuck, who did whatever Pyrs did.

"George, could you walk us through the schedule, please?" said the chairman.

George consulted his tablet where he'd been typing at high speed.

"Certainly, sir. It's 3:15 now. At 3:40 we will all leave the hotel and head to Times Square, with a discreet security escort."

"How are we going to avoid being seen by the media ahead of time?" asked the chairman.

"I'm getting there, sir," said George. "At 3:42, five B-list reality television stars will enter Times Square from the south, at 46th and Seventh. They will be pretending to be drunk—at least I hope they will be pretending—and will provide a distraction for the cameras. While the media's attention is focused elsewhere, we will walk backstage at the north end of Times Square to be in place for the press conference."

"Excellent," said the chairman.

"That's what you pay me the big bucks for, sir." George paused to take a breath, then continued. "At four o'clock, plus thirty seconds for the commentators' lead ins, you will step up to the podium and deliver your opening words."

"Hard copy?"

"Delivered shortly, sir."

"Carry on."

"Then you will introduce Dr. Yu and her family. Dr. Obi, if you and your children could stand to the right and let Dr. Yu stand to your left, next to the chairman, that would be great."

"No problem," said Janet and Anthony, Sr.

"We'd like you to say a few words about your discovery, Janet," said George. "Please keep them at a level Anthony, Jr. can understand."

"Anthony, Jr. can do elementary trigonometry problems and knows how to pronounce the names of more than seventy species of dinosaur," said Janet.

"Please keep your remarks at a level that *I* can understand. And don't mention anything about our three, uh, guests."

"Got it," said Janet.

"I took the liberty of preparing some talking points for you," said George. "Hard copies are being delivered."

"Thanks," said Janet. Then she looked down and realized she was wearing an old pair of jeans and a blue Berkeley sweatshirt. "Wait a second. I can't go on television dressed like this."

"It does make you look like an authentic academic," said George, "but I've got it taken care of."

"I trust you," said Janet. She looked over at her husband and kids who were also dressed rather far toward the casual side of the fashion bell curve. The girls were presentable in complementary Anna and Elsa t-shirts from *Frozen,* and Anthony, Jr. was wearing a clean t-shirt with dinosaur skeletons on it that they'd bought for him at the American Museum of Natural History yesterday. Her husband might need a wardrobe upgrade, though. He was wearing a black *xkcd* t-shirt that read "Stand back: I'm going to try Science" and a light jacket. On second thought, she considered, he was just fine.

"After Janet finishes—you should take five minutes or less—please step back and stand next to your husband."

George turned to the chairman.

"Then it's time for the big reveal. Make the announcement about our invitation to join the Galactic Free Trade Association, then I'll send Chuck, Jannosh and Murriym out on stage to your left. Introduce each of them in turn and then let Chuck have the podium. Be sure to pull the steps out so that Chuck will be tall enough to reach the microphone and be seen."

George shifted to address the Pyr.

"You're up next. Keep it short and sweet. Talk about all the benefits of membership—unlimited energy, the cure for cancer, warp drives—but don't answer any questions. The chairman is going to introduce you as 'Chuck,' not Charles Maurice de Talleyrand-Périgord, so don't let that throw you. We're an informal species."

"Does that work for you?" said the chairman.

"Up to a point," said Chuck. "I have a slide show."

The chairman cringed, but didn't let it show on his face.

"That might be better at a later date," said George.

The chairman nodded enthusiastically.

George heard a soft tapping at the door to the suite and stepped into the hall to take a Bloomingdale's bag from one of the guards and accept a thin manila envelope. He reentered and handed two sheets of paper from the envelope to Chuck and two sheets to Janet. Then he handed the envelope to the chairman, who retreated to one of the suite's four bathrooms to review his hard copies. Janet pointed at the Bloomingdale's bag.

"Is that for me?" she said.

"I said I'd take care of you," said George. "I hope I got your sizes right. Go get changed."

Janet looked in the bag and smiled, then headed for the adult bedroom and waved for her husband to follow her.

"I may need some help getting dressed," she said. Anthony, Sr. followed her and looked at George in a way that said, "You've got the kids."

George sighed, but rolled with it. He carefully pulled two items out of the FedEx Office bag the messenger had brought earlier and gave one to Murriym and one to Jannosh. He was careful to close and reseal the bag.

"Time to get dressed for the press conference," he said.

"Don't I get anything?" asked Chuck.

"You're the wrong shape," said George, who noticed the little alien looked hurt. "But I have something special for you."

George partially opened the FedEx bag and gave Chuck a quick look inside. The little alien appeared delighted.

"That's perfect," said the Pyr, who was starting to look nervous now that his speech to the people of Earth was getting closer. At least that's how George interpreted the Pyr shifting a few inches to the left, then to the right, then forward and back again. Either that or he needed to use the bathroom.

"Do you need an excretion facility?" asked George.

"No, I'm just nervous," said Chuck.

"I'd been meaning to ask you," said George, "does GaFTA have a flag?"

"Nothing official," said Chuck, "we're too individualistic for that. But we sometimes use a black fabric hanging covered in white stars to celebrate milestones in the history of the Association."

"Sounds pretty," said George. "What do you call it?"

"The Star Spangled Banner," said Chuck.

"Something to think about later," said George. "You'd better get dressed."

The girls had been helping their favorite aliens, Jeanette with

Murriym and Elizabeth with Jannosh. Elizabeth had somehow convinced the Nicósn to say "Ho ho ho!" That made all the children giggle in ultrasonics. Anthony, Jr. was fascinated by Chuck's Styrofoam head and insisted on adding eyes to it with a Sharpie. Soon all three aliens were back in their robes, just in time to see Anthony, Sr. and Janet emerge from the bedroom.

Janet was wearing a sharp, coordinated outfit with gray slacks, a white blouse and a navy jacket that looked professional and gave her a gravitas appropriate to the occasion. She was clutching two sheets of paper and looking about as nervous as Chuck, making allowances for differences in anatomy. As she read over her talking points she glanced at George and nodded, acknowledging each point and confirming her agreement.

"This will be a big help," said Janet, waving the papers in George's direction. "I really appreciate it."

"Just remember to smile, keep it short, be yourself, and use a third grade vocabulary," said George. "The media will love you."

"I hope so," said Janet.

"*We* love you, mommy," said her children.

"And I love you, too. Let's do this—and get it over with."

"I wonder if Columbus felt this way when he discovered America?" said Anthony, Sr.

"Columbus was a dope," said Anthony, Jr. "He thought he found China. Boy was *he* wrong."

George knocked on the door to the bathroom where the chairman was reviewing his speech.

"It's time to go, sir."

George heard water running.

"I'll be right with you," said the chairman.

He was out in moments and George—with the FedEx Office bag—herded everyone down the elevator and into their proper marching order. George and the chairman went first, followed by the three aliens and discreetly shadowed by two security guards.

Then there was a gap followed by Dr. Obi and the three children, then Dr. Yu, wearing sensible, but brand new shoes, and wishing she could wear her sneakers. Two more security guards brought up the rear. They waited in the hotel's entryway until George got the signal that the B-list reality television celebrities had arrived.

"Stay casual," whispered George to his charges. "If you do, no one will notice us."

George was right. The camera crews had all headed to the south end of Times Square to watch the B-list screaming match and the three print reporters had their heads down checking their cell phones. George led them expertly into the curtained-off area behind the stage. They had ten minutes before show time. The chairman and Dr. Yu were focused on reviewing their talking points and the security guards outside the curtains ensured that no one else was allowed to enter the backstage area. George took Chuck aside.

"Do you have anything cool and ultra-technological to prove to the people watching the press conference that you're not just audio-animatronics or robots or something? Something that would convince everyone watching that you're real, not fake?"

"I have my diplomatic credentials," said the Pyr. He reached into somewhere and pulled out a small metal disk and handed it to George. "Just touch it."

George did. Music started to play directly in his inner ear.

"It's a world of laughter, a world of tears…"

"What the…?" said George.

"Wrong one," said Chuck, handing George a piece of metal shaped more like a comet or a meteor.

"These credentials authenticate Charles Maurice de Talleyrand-Périgord as an envoy extraordinary and minister plenipotentiary to Earth from the Galactic Free Trade Association with all the rights and privileges inherent thereto," recited a deep basso voice inside George's brain.

"Interesting, but not flashy," said George. "Got anything else?"

Chuck pulled another donut-shaped device from somewhere.

"Just this."

"What is it?"

"My slide show projector."

"Yeah, but we agreed we'd save that for later. Terrans are pretty jaded about slide shows."

"It's cool, though," said Chuck. "It's holographic. Let me set it to a really small size and project it just for the two of us. I included some Earth-specific samples."

Chuck fiddled with the device and suddenly a greenish head the size of a grapefruit appeared between them.

"Do not arouse the wrath of the great and powerful Oz," said the head.

"We were doing stuff like that back in 1939. Anything else?"

"It can make much bigger images."

"You think about it," said George. "It's time to get started. I'll stay backstage with you three where I can help you get out of your robes and let you know when it's time to go on."

"Great," said the Pyr.

Jannosh and Murriym were playing with the girls and Anthony, Jr. was climbing through the maze of crisscrossed pipes that supported the back of the stage.

George checked his watch and touched the chairman's shoulder.

"It's time, sir."

"Right. Wish me luck."

"Good luck. The planet is going to need it."

The chairman stepped through the tall black curtains and approached the podium. He was reasonably confident he'd memorized his lines, but his notes were folded in his breast pocket just in case. A large crowd had gathered in Times Square, unsure what was going to happen, but curious. When the chairman reached the podium he stood up very straight, appreciating that school children would be watching recordings of this moment for the next hundred years. He squared his shoulders, took a deep breath, and began.

"People of Earth," said the chairman, "today is a day that will forever change humankind's place in the universe. It is a day that will always be remembered."

The crowd grew quiet. This wasn't a typical politician's "My fellow Americans," sort of speech or a more traditional "Ladies and gentlemen" introduction.

"The announcement I will soon make is only possible because of the inspired work of a dedicated scientist whose recent breakthrough ranks with the discovery of fire in the history of human civilization."

When the chairman paused, the audience started to clap tentatively, then enthusiastically.

"Let me introduce… Dr. Janet Yu and her family."

The two adults and three children entered the stage and walked to their right to cheers and applause. The crowd didn't know what it was cheering for, but they liked a show.

"Dr. Yu and her husband, Dr. Anthony Obi, both have doctorates in physics from Stanford. Their children are Jeanette, Elizabeth and Anthony, Jr."

The kids waved as their names were mentioned. All five members of the family had nervous smiles.

"Dr. Yu has recently been involved in a DARPA sponsored research study in partnership with Carnegie Mellon University and IBM to develop computer chips with no transmission lag time. We've all been frustrated when our access to the Internet slows down. Dr. Yu's research is designed to address that. It focuses on transmitting signals from Point A to Point B, a thousand miles away, with no slowdown or delay in between. But I'm no scientist, I'm a businessman. Dr. Yu can explain it a lot better herself."

Janet took the podium and the crowd cheered again. At this point, they'd cheer for someone announcing the score in the Yankees game. She pulled the microphone down and spoke into it directly.

"Unaccustomed as I am to public speaking," she began.

The audience laughed sympathetically.

"Since I'm a research scientist and spend most of my time in basement labs…"

More laughs.

"I'll just have to put things in plain and simple terms. Last Friday afternoon, my team and I created a congruency—a wormhole connecting two widely separated points in space as if there was no distance between them."

There were a few gasps from more knowledgeable members of the crowd and the chairman noticed the print reporters typing at high speed.

"That means the end of slow Internet connections, no delays and no clogged pipes. Every connected device can be just one hop away from the cloud."

Several younger members of the crowd started whistling and cheering loudly. Gamers, Janet guessed. They understood what her research meant.

"Unfortunately," said Janet, "my grant was canceled by Congressional budget cutbacks less than an hour and a half after my team's discovery, so I don't have more to tell you."

The chairman kept a smile on his face but winced inside. That wasn't in the script. Dr. Yu's slam would cost him big time. He'd have to open the bank's wallet to smooth things over with substantial political contributions. On the other hand, he didn't really care. After today, he and JPMorgan Chase were sure to become even richer.

"Now it's time for me to pass the baton back to our host who will tell you what my team's discovery really means for our planet."

Dr. Yu stepped back, shook the chairman's hand, and walked over to stand with her family. The chairman returned to the podium and leaned down.

"Earlier this afternoon I learned that we are not alone. Prompted by Dr. Yu's discovery, three non-humans teleported into my office and invited the business community of Earth to join the Galactic Free Trade Association."

"April Fools!" shouted someone near the front of the crowd.

"No, this is not an April Fool's Day joke. I'm absolutely serious—this is a tremendous opportunity for our planet. The Galactic Free Trade Association is offering us unlimited, almost free energy, cures for cancer and faster than light travel. And that's just the beginning."

The crowd didn't know how to react. Some cheered. Some laughed. Some even booed.

"But you don't have to believe me. You can hear the invitation directly from the Association representatives who made First Contact. Please welcome Chuck, the leader of their diplomatic delegation."

There was scattered clapping and more booing. Backstage, Chuck looked at George for reassurance. George opened the FedEx Office bag and gave Chuck a yellow smiley-face balloon.

"They'll love you," said George, pushing the little alien onto the stage.

The chairman pulled out all the steps from underneath the podium and met Chuck, shaking a tentacle in passing. When the crowd saw the balloon held by a grinning four foot pyramid-shaped alien, they clapped and cheered and whistled, with only a few scattered boos. Chuck climbed the steps and addressed the assembly.

"Hi folks," he said. "My name's Chuck. I'm part of a species called Pyrs. We're really good at math. Let me introduce the other members of my delegation."

The next alien came on stage.

"Ladies first," said Chuck. "This is Murriym. She's a Tigrammath and she doesn't play basketball, but I hear the WNBA is interested."

The crowd went wild and clapped and cheered. Murriym was wearing a white "I LOVE NEW YORK" t-shirt with a large red heart. She bowed, then straightened up to her full height and faked a jump shot. The clapping and cheering got even louder.

George sent out the last alien. The crowd was laughing now.

"If NASCAR can do it, so can we," said Chuck. George had arranged the perfect sponsorship deal for the red-skinned, white-bearded Nicósn who looked like Santa Claus. He was wearing a red t-shirt with the Coca-Cola script logo on it in large white letters. "This here's Jannosh," said Chuck. "He's a Nicósn from the planet Nicós, and just to show you that we're business beings, not politicians, he has a little something to say."

Jannosh came to the podium and stood next to Chuck. Murriym stood on the other side to provide a perfect photo op when Jannosh leaned in and said, "Hey, everybody! I want you to know... We're the Real Thing."

The crowd bubbled with laughter.

Then Chuck triggered his slide projector and a giant yellow smiley face appeared to float above Times Square. Images started pouring in from the other side of the planet and were displayed on the jumbo screens above the stage. A similar giant smiley face had appeared on the surface of the Moon.

The cheering lasted for seventeen full minutes.

* * * * *

George and the chairman stood close together on the other side of the stage from the Obi-Yu family.

"The little pyramid suckered us," said the chairman.

"Not really," said George, "though he is a natural. The two t-shirts were my idea. The mayor insisted on the first one."

"Brilliant," said the chairman.

"I know, right?" said George. "The balloon was my idea, too. But Chuck figured out that last bit all on his own."

The two men looked out at the cheering crowd and then glanced up at the eight-story screen above their heads showing a smiling Moon.

"You'll go down in history as the man who sold the earth on joining the Galactics," said George.

"You did more to make that happen than I did," said the chairman. "I hope you know I'm giving you a big raise."

"I thought you might," said George, "but I'm giving my notice as soon as we get back to the office."

"You're leaving me?"

"Don't be a baby," said George. "You knew it was going to happen sometime. Dr. Yu and Dr. Obi offered to make me the president of the new company they're forming to develop congruent technologies."

"I'll back you," said the chairman.

"I'm counting on it," said George. "Now let's get these hams off the stage and start negotiating what their deal is *really* about."

"Sounds like a plan," said the chairman. "Sounds like a plan."

* * * * *

From the 19th floor of the New York Marriott Marquis, in a room overlooking Times Square, a Pâkk and a human stood together looking down on the celebration.

"Nicely done," said the Pâkk.

"Thanks," said the human. "Now the fun begins."

About the Author

Dave Schroeder is a former Chief Information Officer who's done his share of tech support. He's served as Chief Technology Officer for a Bay Area dotcom and led the ecommerce division of a major Internet consulting company. He also wrote the book, lyrics and music for *Softwear.com,* a musical comedy produced off-off-Broadway. Dave lives in suburban Atlanta where he enjoys writing and voice acting with the Atlanta Radio Theatre Company.

Adventures in the
Galactic Free Trade Association
universe continue in:

Xenotech Rising

Xenotech Queen's Gambit

and

Xenotech What Happens

soon to be followed by

Xenotech General Mayhem
coming in Q4 2016

Sign up for the Xenotech Support mailing list at
XenotechSupport.com to get advance notice
of new publications and receive a link to a
bonus short story.

www.ingramcontent.com/pod-product-compliance
Lightning Source LLC
Chambersburg PA
CBHW071224130626
46555CB00004B/1834